Railway Series, No. 4

TANK ENGINE THOMAS AGAIN

by

THE REV. W. AWDRY

with illustrations by

C. REGINALD DALBY

KAYE & WARD LIMITED

First published by
Edmund Ward (Publishers) Ltd 1949
Fifteenth impression by Kaye & Ward Ltd
The Windmill Press, Kingswood, Tadworth, Surrey
1981

Copyright 1949 Edmund Ward (Publishers) Ltd
Copyright © 1970 Kaye & Ward Ltd

ISBN 0 7182 0003 9

Printed and bound in Great Britain by
William Clowes (Beccles) Limited, Beccles and London

Dear Friends,

Here is news from Thomas's branch line. It is clearly no ordinary line, and life on it is far from dull.

Thomas asks me to say that, if you are ever in the Region, you must be sure to visit him and travel on his line. "They will have never seen anything like it," he says proudly.

I know I haven't!

THE AUTHOR

Thomas and the Guard

THOMAS THE TANK ENGINE is very proud of his branch line. He thinks it is the most important part of the whole railway.

He has two coaches. They are old, and need new paint, but he loves them very much. He calls them Annie and Clarabel. Annie can only take passengers, but Clarabel can take passengers, luggage and the Guard.

As they run backwards and forwards along the line, Thomas sings them little songs, and Annie and Clarabel sing too.

When Thomas starts from a station he sings, "Oh, come along! We're rather late. Oh, come along! We're rather late." And the coaches sing, "We're coming along, we're coming along."

They don't mind what Thomas says to them because they know he is trying to please the Fat Controller; and they know, too, that if Thomas is cross, he is not cross with them.

He is cross with the engines on the main line who have made him late.

One day they had to wait for Henry's train. It was late. Thomas was getting crosser and crosser. "How can I run my line properly if Henry is always late? He doesn't realize that the Fat Controller depends on ME," and he whistled impatiently.

At last Henry came.

"Where have you been, lazybones?" asked Thomas crossly.

"Oh dear, my system is out of order; no one understands my case. You don't know what I suffer," moaned Henry.

"Rubbish!" said Thomas, "you're too fat; you need exercise!"

Lots of people with piles of luggage got out of Henry's train, and they all climbed into Annie and Clarabel. Thomas had to wait till they were ready. At last the Guard blew his whistle, and Thomas started at once.

The Guard turned round to jump into his van, tripped over an old lady's umbrella, and fell flat on his face.

By the time he had picked himself up, Thomas and Annie and Clarabel were steaming out of the station.

"Come along! Come along!" puffed Thomas, but Clarabel didn't want to come. "I've lost my nice Guard, I've lost my nice Guard," she sobbed. Annie tried to tell Thomas "We haven't a Guard, we haven't a Guard," but he was hurrying, and wouldn't listen.

"Oh, come along! Oh, come along!" he puffed impatiently.

Annie and Clarabel tried to put on their brakes, but they couldn't without the Guard.

"Where is our Guard? Where is our Guard?" they cried. Thomas didn't stop till they came to a signal.

"Bother that signal!" said Thomas. "What's the matter?"

"I don't know," said his Driver. "The Guard will tell us in a minute." They waited and waited, but the Guard didn't come.

"Peep peep peep peep! Where is the Guard?" whistled Thomas.

"We've left him behind," sobbed Annie and Clarabel together. The Driver, the Fireman and the passengers looked, and there was the Guard running as fast as he could along the line, with his flags in one hand and his whistle in the other.

Everybody cheered him. He was very hot, so he sat down and had a drink and told them all about it.

"I'm very sorry, Mr Guard," said Thomas.

"It wasn't your fault, Thomas; it was the old lady's umbrella. Look, the signal is down; let's make up for lost time."

Annie and Clarabel were so pleased to have their Guard again, that they sang, "As fast as you like, as fast as you like!" to Thomas, all the way, and they reached the end of the line quicker than ever before.

Thomas goes Fishing

THOMAS's branch line had a station by a river. As he rumbled over the bridge, he would see people fishing. Sometimes they stood quietly by their lines; sometimes they were actually jerking fish out of the water.

Thomas often wanted to stay and watch, but his Driver said, "No! what would the Fat Controller say if we were late?"

Thomas thought it would be lovely to stop by the river. "I should like to go fishing," he said to himself longingly.

Every time he met another engine he would say "I want to fish." They all answered "Engines don't go fishing."

"Silly stick-in-the-muds!" he would snort impatiently.

Thomas generally had to take in water at the station by the river. One day he stopped as usual, and his Fireman put the pipe from the water tower in his tank. Then he turned the tap, but it was out of order and no water came.

"Bother!" said Thomas, "I am thirsty."

"Never mind," said his Driver, "we'll get some water from the river."

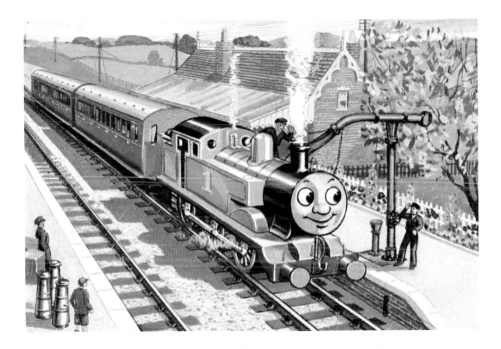

They found a bucket and some rope, and went to the bridge, then the Driver let the bucket down to the water.

The bucket was old, and had five holes, so they had to fill it, pull it up, and empty it into Thomas's tank as quickly as they could.

"There's a hole in my bucket, dear Liza, dear Liza," sang the Fireman.

"Never mind about Liza," said the Driver, "you empty that bucket, before you spill the water over me!"

They finished at last. "That's good! That's good!" puffed Thomas as he started, and Annie and Clarabel ran happily behind.

They puffed along the valley, and were in the tunnel when Thomas began to feel a pain in his boiler, while steam hissed from his safety valve in an alarming way.

"There's too much steam," said his Driver, and his Fireman opened the tap in the feed pipe, to let more water into the boiler, but none came.

"Oh, dear," groaned Thomas, "I'm going to burst! I'm going to burst!"

They damped down his fire, and struggled on.

"I've got such a pain, I've got such a pain," Thomas hissed.

Just outside the last station they stopped, uncoupled Annie and Clarabel and ran Thomas, who was still hissing fit to burst, on a siding right out of the way.

Then while the Guard telephoned for an Engine Inspector, and the Fireman was putting out the fire, the Driver wrote notices in large letters which he hung on Thomas in front and behind, "DANGER! KEEP AWAY."

Soon the Inspector and the Fat Controller arrived. "Cheer up, Thomas!" they said. "We'll soon put you right."

The Driver told them what had happened. "So the feed pipe is blocked," said the Inspector. "I'll just look in the tanks."

He climbed up and peered in, then he came down. "Excuse me, sir," he said to the Fat Controller, "please look in the tank and tell me what you see."

"Certainly, Inspector." He clambered up, looked in and nearly fell off in surprise.

"Inspector," he whispered, "can *you* see *fish* ?"

"Gracious goodness me!" said the Fat Controller, "how did the fish get there, Driver?"

Thomas's Driver scratched his head, "We must have fished them from the river," and he told them about the bucket.

The Fat Controller laughed, "Well, Thomas, so you and your Driver have been fishing, but fish don't suit you, and we must get them out."

So the Driver and the Fireman fetched rods and nets, and they all took turns at fishing in Thomas's tank, while the Fat Controller told them how to do it.

When they had caught all the fish, the Station Master gave them some potatoes, the Driver borrowed a frying-pan, while the Fireman made a fire beside the line and did the cooking.

Then they all had a lovely picnic supper of fish and chips.

"That was good," said the Fat Controller as he finished his share, "but fish don't suit you, Thomas, so you mustn't do it again."

"No, sir, I won't," said Thomas sadly, "engines don't go fishing, it's too uncomfortable."

Thomas, Terence and the Snow

Autumn was changing the leaves from green to brown. The fields were changing too, from yellow stubble to brown earth.

As Thomas puffed along, he heard the "chug chug chug" of a tractor at work.

One day, stopping for a signal, he saw the tractor close by.

"Hullo!" said the tractor, "I'm Terence; I'm ploughing."

"I'm Thomas; I'm pulling a train. What ugly wheels you've got."

"They're not ugly, they're caterpillars," said Terence. "I can go anywhere; *I* don't need rails."

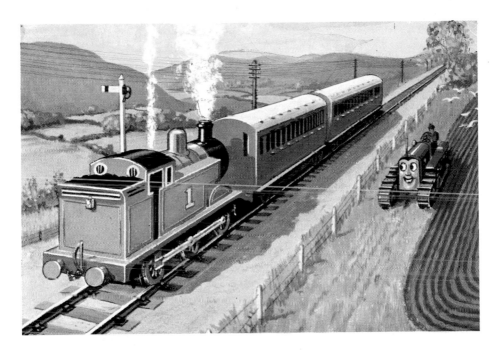

"I don't want to go anywhere," said Thomas huffily, "I like my rails, thank you!"

Thomas often saw Terence working, but though he whistled, Terence never answered.

Winter came, and with it dark heavy clouds full of snow.

"I don't like it," said Thomas's Driver. "A heavy fall is coming. I hope it doesn't stop us."

"Pooh!" said Thomas, seeing the snow melt on the rails, "soft stuff, nothing to it!" And he puffed on feeling cold, but confident.

They finished their journey safely; but the

country was covered, and the rails were two dark lines standing out in the white snow.

"You'll need your Snow Plough for the next journey, Thomas," said his Driver.

"Pooh! Snow is silly soft stuff—it won't stop me."

"Listen to me," his Driver replied, "we are going to fix your Snow Plough on, and I want no nonsense, please."

The Snow Plough was heavy and uncomfortable and made Thomas cross. He shook it, and he banged it and when they got back it was so damaged that the Driver had to take it off.

"You're a very naughty engine," said his Driver, as he shut the shed door that night.

Next morning, both Driver and Fireman came early and worked hard to mend the Snow Plough; but they couldn't make it fit properly.

It was time for the first train. Thomas was pleased, "I shan't have to wear it, I shan't have to wear it," he puffed to Annie and Clarabel.

"I hope it's all right, I hope it's all right," they whispered anxiously to each other.

The Driver was anxious, too. "It's not bad here," he said to the Fireman, "but it's sure to be deep in the valley."

It was snowing again when Thomas started, but the rails were not covered.

"Silly soft stuff! Silly soft stuff!" he puffed. "I didn't need that stupid old thing yesterday; I shan't today. Snow can't stop me," and he rushed into the tunnel, thinking how clever he was.

At the other end he saw a heap of snow fallen from the sides of the cutting.

"Silly old snow," said Thomas, and charged it.

"Cinders and ashes!" said Thomas, "I'm stuck!"—and he was!

"Back! Thomas, back!" said his Driver. Thomas tried, but his wheels spun, and he couldn't move.

More snow fell and piled up round him.

The Guard went back for help, while the Driver, Fireman and passengers tried to dig the snow away; but, as fast as they dug, more snow slipped down until Thomas was nearly buried.

"Oh, my wheels and coupling rods!" said Thomas sadly, "I shall have to stop here till I'm frozen. What a silly engine I am," and Thomas began to cry.

At last, a tooting in the distance told them a 'bus had come for the passengers.

Then Terence chugged through the tunnel.

He pulled the empty coaches away, and came back for Thomas. Thomas's wheels were clear, but still spun helplessly when he tried to move.

Terence tugged and slipped, and slipped and tugged, and at last dragged Thomas into the tunnel.

"Thank you, Terence, your caterpillars are splendid," said Thomas gratefully.

"I hope you'll be sensible now, Thomas," said his Driver severely.

"I'll try," said Thomas, as he puffed home.

Thomas and Bertie

ONE day Thomas was waiting at the junction, when a 'bus came into the yard.

"Hullo!" said Thomas, "who are you?"

"I'm Bertie, who are you?"

"I'm Thomas; I run this line."

"So you're Thomas. Ah—I remember now, you stuck in the snow, I took your passengers and Terence pulled you out. I've come to help you with your passengers today."

"Help me!" said Thomas crossly, going bluer than ever and letting off steam. "I can go faster than you."

"You can't."

"I can."

"I'll race you," said Bertie.

Their Drivers agreed. The Station Master said, "Are you ready?—Go!" and they were off.

Thomas never could go fast at first, and Bertie drew in front. Thomas was running well but he did not hurry.

"Why don't you go fast? Why don't you go fast?" called Annie and Clarabel anxiously.

"Wait and see, wait and see," hissed Thomas.

"He's a long way ahead, a long way ahead," they wailed, but Thomas didn't mind. He remembered the Level Crossing.

There was Bertie fuming at the gates while they sailed gaily through.

"Goodbye, Bertie," called Thomas.

The road left the railway and went through a village, so they couldn't see Bertie.

They stopped at the station. "Peep pip peep! Quickly, please!" called Thomas. Everybody got out quickly, the Guard whistled and off they went.

"Come along! Come along!" sang Thomas.

"We're coming along! We're coming along!", sang Annie and Clarabel.

"Hurry! Hurry! Hurry!" panted Thomas, looking straight ahead.

Then he whistled shrilly in horror, for Bertie was crossing the bridge over the railway, tooting triumphantly on his horn!

"Oh, deary me! Oh, deary me!" groaned Thomas.

"He's a long way in front, a long way in front," wailed Annie and Clarabel.

"Steady, Thomas," said his Driver, "we'll beat Bertie yet."

"We'll beat Bertie yet; we'll beat Bertie yet," echoed Annie and Clarabel.

"We'll do it; we'll do it," panted Thomas bravely. "Oh, bother, there's a station."

As he stopped, he heard a toot.

"Goodbye, Thomas, you must be tired. Sorry I can't stop, we 'buses have to work you know. Goodbye!"

The next station was by the river. They got there quickly, but the signal was up.

"Oh, dear," thought Thomas, "we've lost!"

But he felt better after a drink. Then James rattled through with a goods train, and the signal dropped, showing the line was clear.

"Hurrah, we're off! Hurrah, we're off!" puffed Thomas gaily.

As they rumbled over the bridge they heard an impatient "Toot, Toot," and there was Bertie waiting at the red light, while cars and lorries crossed the narrow bridge in the opposite direction.

Road and railway ran up the valley side by side, a stream tumbling between.

Thomas had not crossed the bridge when Bertie started with a roar, and soon shot ahead. Excited passengers in train and 'bus cheered and shouted across the valley. Now Thomas reached his full speed and foot by foot, yard by yard he gained, till they were running level. Bertie tried hard, but Thomas was too fast; slowly but surely he drew ahead, till whistling triumphantly he plunged into the tunnel, leaving Bertie toiling far behind.

"I've done it! I've done it," panted Thomas in the tunnel.

"We've done it, hooray! We've done it, hooray!" chanted Annie and Clarabel; and whistling proudly, they whoooshed out of the tunnel into the last station.

The passengers gave Thomas "three cheers" and told the Station Master and the Porters all about the race. When Bertie came in they gave him "three cheers" too.

"Well done, Thomas," said Bertie. "That was fun, but to beat you over that hill I should have to grow wings and be an aeroplane."

Thomas and Bertie now keep each other very busy. Bertie finds people in the villages who want to go by train, and takes them to Thomas; while Thomas brings people to the station for Bertie to take home.

They often talk about their race. But Bertie's passengers don't like being bounced like peas in a frying-pan! And the Fat Controller has warned Thomas about what happens to engines who race at dangerous speeds.

So although (between you and me) they would like to have another race, I don't think they ever will.

The Reverend W. Awdry's Railway Series

RAILWAY MAP

A full-colour, laminated map showing where Thomas the Tank Engine and his friends live and work. Designed by Peter Edwards, it shows the layout of the Fat and Thin Controllers' Railways on the Island of Sodor. When open it measures $21 \times 33\frac{1}{2}$ in.

SURPRISE PACKET

Designed and drawn by Peter Edwards with the Reverend Awdry the *Surprise Packet* is full of stories, games, puzzles, things to make and things to do ($11\frac{1}{2} \times 11\frac{1}{2}$ in., 12 sheets printed in full-colour and black-and-white, and bound into a laminated portfolio).

RECORDS

The first eight books in the series, narrated by Johnny Morris, are available on four L.P. records (or cassettes). Six further books read by William Rushton are available on three L.P.'s (or cassettes) all from Decca/Argo.

PUZZLES

Puzzles featuring Thomas the Tank Engine and his friends are now available from Whitman Publishing (U.K.) Ltd. Each puzzle is printed in full-colour, made up of 30 large wooden pieces in boxes or 54 large card pieces in new, sturdy drums.